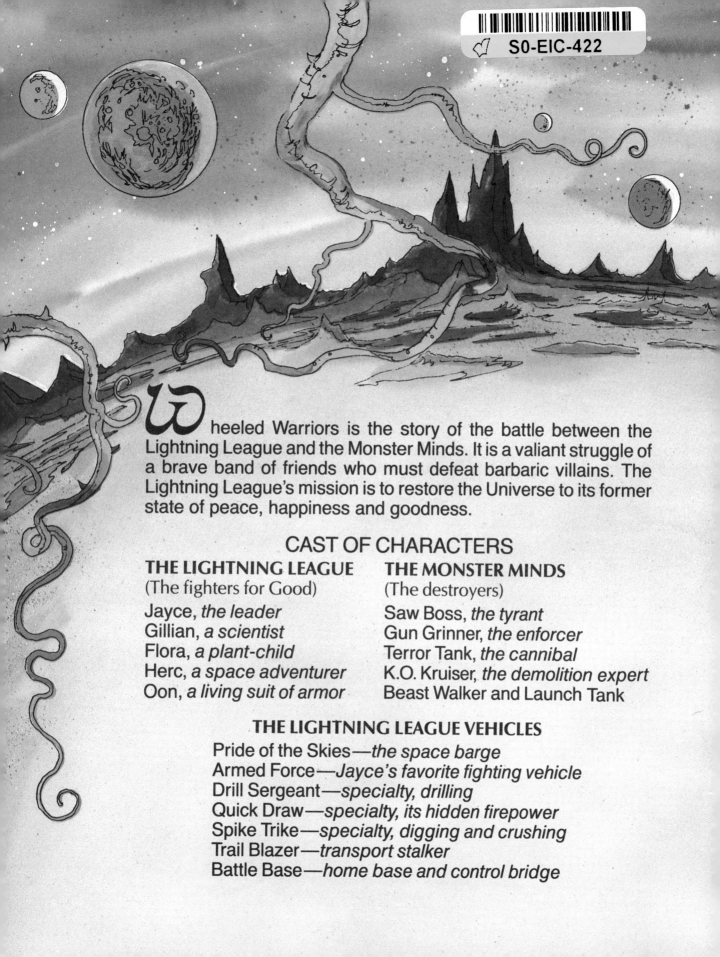

Wheeled Warriors is the story of the battle between the Lightning League and the Monster Minds. It is a valiant struggle of a brave band of friends who must defeat barbaric villains. The Lightning League's mission is to restore the Universe to its former state of peace, happiness and goodness.

CAST OF CHARACTERS

THE LIGHTNING LEAGUE
(The fighters for Good)

Jayce, *the leader*
Gillian, *a scientist*
Flora, *a plant-child*
Herc, *a space adventurer*
Oon, *a living suit of armor*

THE MONSTER MINDS
(The destroyers)

Saw Boss, *the tyrant*
Gun Grinner, *the enforcer*
Terror Tank, *the cannibal*
K.O. Kruiser, *the demolition expert*
Beast Walker and Launch Tank

THE LIGHTNING LEAGUE VEHICLES

Pride of the Skies—*the space barge*
Armed Force—*Jayce's favorite fighting vehicle*
Drill Sergeant—*specialty, drilling*
Quick Draw—*specialty, its hidden firepower*
Spike Trike—*specialty, digging and crushing*
Trail Blazer—*transport stalker*
Battle Base—*home base and control bridge*

THE ADVENTURES BEGIN

A GOLDEN BOOK
Western Publishing Company, Inc.
Racine, Wisconsin 53404

Library of Congress Catalog Card Number: 85-070075
ISBN 0-932631-10-X

A B C D E F G H I J

Something very strange had happened to the Universe. One planet after another was being attacked by vines that reached out and took hold in their soil. These vines became roadways through space, and weird plant-machines used them to invade and destroy the planets. The invaders were known as the Monster Minds.

Only one small band of heroes opposed the Monster Minds. The group was called the Lightning League and their leader was a nineteen-year-old young man named Jayce.

Jayce had been testing Armed Force, one of Gillian's inventions. "Gillian, you may have made this vehicle for my father," he said into the radio, "but I was born to drive it."

Suddenly Jayce heard an ominous sound. He heard the noise of something trampling the ground, then the roar of a machine. He knew what was charging through the woods.

"Monster Minds!" he exclaimed, as K.O. Kruiser, Terror Tank and Gun Grinner bolted into view.

"Stop him!" commanded Gun Grinner.

"And save the scraps for me!" snarled Terror Tank. "I haven't eaten metal all day!"

K.O. Kruiser, whose dull-witted brain knew no fear, attacked first. "Enough talk!" he roared, as he swung his heavy wrecking ball at Jayce's machine.

Jayce acted quickly and gunned Armed Force's engine, moving fast enough to escape K.O. Kruiser's blow. "Just a few dents," Jayce thought, as he maneuvered Armed Force away from his foe.

Jayce survived the first attack and sped ahead. The other two Monster Minds vehicles were in close pursuit.

"Blast his machine to junk!" bellowed Terror Tank. "I'm hungry and I crave metal!"

Taking advantage of his head start, Jayce maneuvered Armed Force into a quick turn. He managed to get close enough to overturn Terror Tank while Gun Grinner continued firing his lasers.

The partial defeat of Terror Tank gave Jayce enough time to get away. "We'll continue this party some other time!" Jayce called out.

While K.O. Kruiser and Gun Grinner set Terror Tank back on his wheels, Armed Force bounded away over the rugged terrain.

"I'd sure like to own you, Armed Force," Jayce said to himself, "if you get me back to Gillian's garden."

There was only one place on the entire planet where
the Lightning League was safe from the Monster Minds.
That was Gillian's garden, with its protective dome.

"If I can just reach the garden before the Monster
Minds catch us, I'll be safe," Jayce thought, but the
pursuing Monster Minds kept rolling at top speed.

Gillian had put the last equipment into his newest invention—the Lightning League Battle Base, when he saw Jayce speeding toward the garden.

Flora, the little girl grown from one of the garden's flowers, saw Jayce, too. "Hurry up, Jayce! Hurry!" she cried.

Oon, a living, thinking, talking, eating suit of armor, rattled nervously, clutching his lance.

9

Armed Force passed easily through the energy dome, which was composed of Gillian's ethereal light. It was a wavelength that the Monster Minds could not break through.

Jayce screeched Armed Force to a stop.

"You handle Armed Force like an expert, Jayce," said Gillian. "I built the machine for your father, Audric, but since he is not here to drive it, it is yours. Soon I will give you another gift, one with great power!"

As Jayce thought about the second gift, the news of the defeat of three Monster Minds was being sent to another planet. This once beautiful planet was now the home base of these plant-machines, machines that could think and talk.

Here, amid a tangle of weeds and vines, was the throne room of the leader of the Monster Minds. His name was Saw Boss.

Saw Boss sat on his throne. His headquarters had once been a place where great experiments were made. It was in this very place that Saw Boss and the other Monster Minds had been created. Only in this chamber, away from the dark energies outside, could these plant-beings take on humanoid forms.

"Three of my finest warriors have failed to capture the son of my most hated foe, Audric!" Saw Boss roared.

Saw Boss decided to take care of matters himself, so he walked outside on his rootlike legs. As he passed through the weird black energies, he changed into his vehicular form.

Then Saw Boss rolled to one of the living vines that connected his planet to another of the Monster Minds' planets.

As Saw Boss moved along the highway of vines toward Jayce's planet, a space barge, the Pride of the Skies, was headed in the same direction.

The old ship had seen better days. As its mighty engines coughed, Captain Herc Stormsailor pleaded, "C'mon, baby, don't conk out on me now!"

The barge ship jerked as the engines began to fail. Herc desperately worked the controls, but the ship kept plunging.

"At this moment," he complained, thinking of the cargo stored in his ship, "I could make a fortune selling these supplies to the high-tech market on Planet TG-6…if only I could land there!"

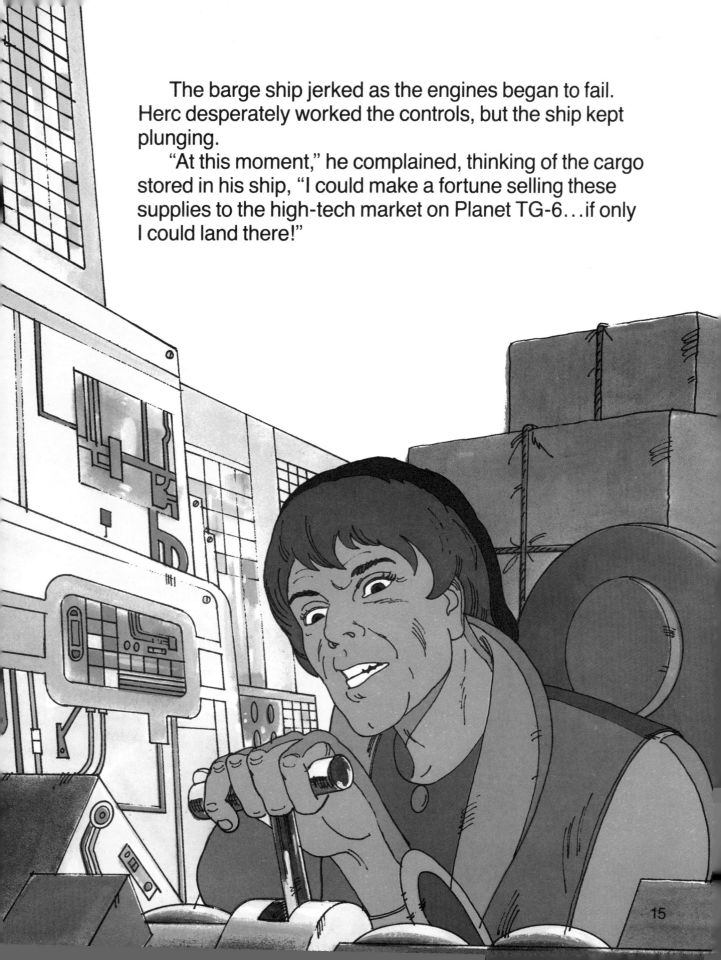

Herc didn't think things could get worse. But they did. Something from outside was stopping the barge's plunge.

Herc had never heard of the Monster Minds' gigantic skyway of vines, but he yelled at them.

"I don't know what you are, but you're not playin' spider and fly with me, you tangled web."

With the fuel left in his ship's reserve tank, Herc Stormsailor burst free!

The space barge came down fast. But it was slowed down by Gillian, who had spotted it in time to turn on a device that controlled gravity. The barge bumped to a halt.

"Careful," said Oon, his metal visor clattering. "There may be a monster in there!"

"Or someone who needs our help," said Jayce.

17

"Oh, it's a human—and I don't think he's hurt," said
Flora with delight. Herc was freed from his damaged ship
and taken to Gillian's house.

"This fruit drink you whipped up made me feel better,
Gillian," said Herc. "Thanks. But tell me—what were
those weird things that grabbed hold of my ship?"

"Monster Mind vines," Jayce replied. "My father, Audric, had tried to increase the galaxy's food supply. He experimented with many new plants hoping to find perfect ones to help people.

"His intentions were good, but something terrible happened.

"A distant star exploded—a star containing strange energies and elements."

"Radiation from that explosion had a bad effect on my father's new plants." Jayce went on. "The plants absorbed those energies and changed into monstrous forms. These plants grew their own intelligent brains. Then they grew into ugly shapes, and became heavily armed vehicles."

"You're space-jivin' me, kid!" laughed Herc. "Machines don't grow. Uh — do they?"

"Well, Dad discovered a way to combat the 'Monster Minds,'" Jayce said. "He developed two roots. Each gave off rays that the Monster Minds could not stand. Dad hoped to produce many more plants with the roots.

"But before he could graft the two roots, the Monster Minds discovered what he intended to do, and they tried to capture him."

"Audric, dressed as a beggar, got away—but first he told Oon what to do. Oon was to find me and give me one of the roots for safekeeping. Dad knew I was here with Gillian.

"By the time Oon got to Gillian's garden, the Monster Minds had spread across the whole galaxy.

"They keep spreading and their vines grabbed your ship."

"That's a wild story, kid," said Herc. "But then, I've seen some weird stuff in this universe."

"Jayce speaks the truth," Gillian said. "His father is lost somewhere, but there is a gift from him that will help us look for him. It is a ring. Here, Jayce, it is now yours."

"A ring? Dad never mentioned a ring!" exclaimed Jayce.

Jayce took the ring from Gillian. It felt warm on Jayce's finger, as if it had a wonderful power. Suddenly, it glowed, and Jayce stared at it in wonder.

"Maybe this ring will help me find my dad, and then we'll graft the roots and we will stop the Monster Minds— for good!" Jayce said.

Gillian smiled and nodded, "Perhaps."

"Herc," Jayce said, "I decided to get some help in my search for Dad. Gillian, Flora and Oon joined me. We became a league opposing the Monster Minds. We call ourselves the Lightning League, and our motto is:

"'A Courageous Heart, A Righteous Quest.'"

"Umm, uh," said Herc. "Are you wanting me to join you, too? Well I don't work unless I am paid..."

"We'll pay you," Jayce agreed.

"In that case, I'll help," and Herc joined the Lightning League.

25

Gillian checked the space barge for damage, and then he had his robots make the repairs. In return for the repairs, Herc agreed to share his cargo and food supplies, which would last for a long time.

When the work was finished and the barge was ready for traveling, Gillian suggested that they take the new Battle Base aboard. It would become their home base in space and also the control bridge for the barge.

Cheers sounded as the mighty vehicle moved aboard!

By the time Saw Boss reached the planet where Jayce was, his three main henchmen—Gun Grinner, K.O. Kruiser and the always hungry Terror Tank—were waiting for him. "We are sorry we failed, master," said K.O. Kruiser. "When do we strike again?"

"Soon, but first, we wait for just the right moment!" sneered their angry leader.

While Saw Boss waited to attack, Gillian worked hard to make good his promise to meet Herc's price. Gillian really wanted Herc in the Lightning League, and so he made one experiment after another, using his magical powers to change lead into gold.

At last, Gillian succeeded! He called Herc to his
laboratory and handed him the artificially created gold.
"You just got yourself one loyal Lightning Leaguer!"
Herc cried out with joy.
"I just hope that gold lasts long enough for Herc to
spend it," Gillian whispered to the armored Oon.

The gold was unstable, but it held its new form very well while the final repairs were made on Herc's barge.

The Battle Base was ready to serve as the control room for the Pride of the Skies. Gillian was concerned about one thing, however.

"The energy dome that covers the garden could interfere with the energies put out by the barge," he said. "It is risky, but I will have to switch off the dome so we can lift off."

Gillian worked the controls that powered the dome. Knowing there was no choice, he slowly shut down the power.

Moments later, the light disappeared. After the dome vanished, something big thundered out of the woods. It was a huge machine like the Lightning League Battle Base…and it had its own crafty brain! It was the Monster Minds' Launch Tank!

The angry Saw Boss, followed by Terror Tank and K.O. Kruiser, sped out of the huge Launch Tank machine.

"Stop that barge," snarled Saw Boss. "Capture them. They must never leave this planet! Ever!"

"Nothing can stop the Monster Minds now," thought Saw Boss. "We'll smash through the barge and then it can't take off. Jayce and his father will never graft those roots."

Inside the Battle Base, cameras showed pictures of the Monster Minds in action. Jayce rushed to Armed Force and took the lead. "Hurry to your machines," he called to the others. "In our vehicles we can defend ourselves against those dreadful plant things."

Immediately, Gillian, Flora and Oon rushed to their vehicles, and Herc warmed up the barge's engines.

Saw Boss attacked first. His giant saw began spinning as he headed toward Armed Force. "Now we meet, son of Audric!" he roared. But speed was on Jayce's side. He drove Armed Force fast enough to miss the spinning saw. Jayce watched as the saw hit a boulder and sliced it in two.

"You won't escape a second time!" yelled Saw Boss.

"That so?" grinned Jayce. "This battle's not over!"

The other Lightning League members in their machines followed Jayce out of the Battle Base. Of the group, Gillian was the one who did not like to drive the machines. He would rather spend his time inventing good things, but now he knew he had to drive Spike Trike. Before Gun Grinner could get him in a bad spot, Gillian drove under Gun Grinner and pushed him over.

Oon did not like battles for reasons of his own. He liked to talk about them, not be a part of them.

His armor clanking, Oon drove Drill Sergeant straight ahead toward Terror Tank. He had no other choice, especially with Flora there to see him.

"I'm gonna eat your armor and that stupid lance!" Terror Tank threatened. But he did not make good his boast.

Little Flora drove the vehicle called Quick Draw, and she was a good warrior. Despite her age and size, she knew how to handle the big machine.

As K.O. Kruiser charged, swinging his heavy wrecking ball, Flora raised Quick Draw's laser rifles. Before the ball could hit her machine, Flora fired defensively—stopping the weapon in mid-swing.

"What's the matter?" she laughed.

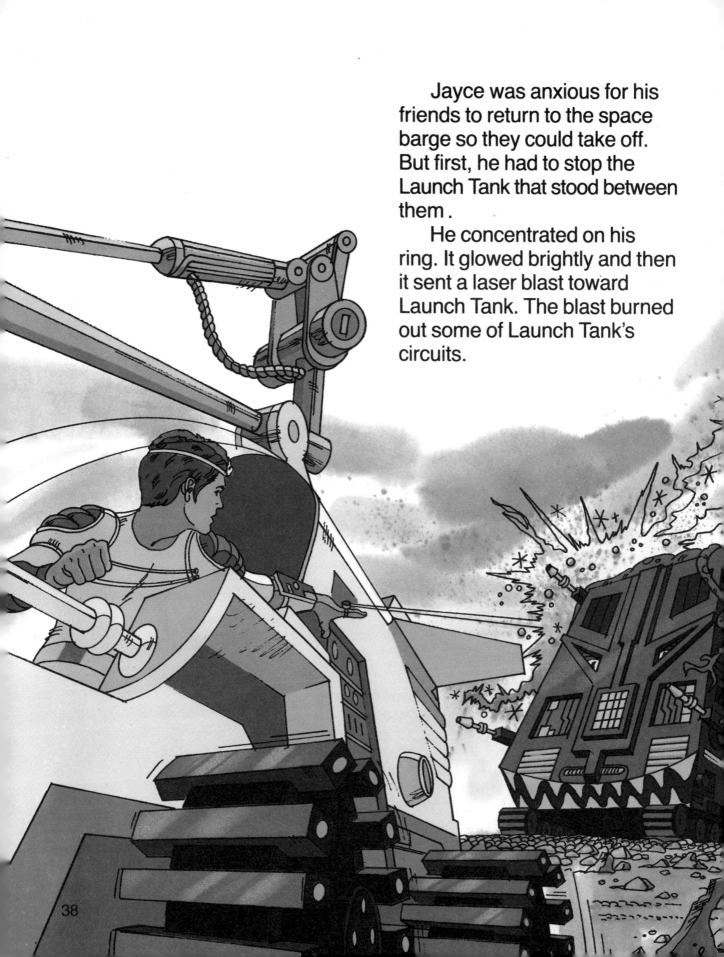

Jayce was anxious for his friends to return to the space barge so they could take off. But first, he had to stop the Launch Tank that stood between them.

He concentrated on his ring. It glowed brightly and then it sent a laser blast toward Launch Tank. The blast burned out some of Launch Tank's circuits.

Saw Boss was mad, as he watched Launch Tank
slowing down. "Stop fighting," he called to his henchmen.
"Get to Launch Tank and begin repairs at once."
As the Monster Minds followed Saw Boss, Jayce
yelled to his friends, "Now! Hurry! The space barge is
ready to lift off as soon as we are aboard."

The battle was over for
now, and the Lightning League
returned to the Pride of the
Skies.

The engines roared. Then
the big craft rose from Gillian's
garden and soared off into
space.

It was later that Herc
Stormsailor looked at his gold.
"Hey!" he shouted. "Who's the
wise guy who switched my gold
for this…this *lead*?!"

"Gillian will make it up to you someday," Flora said, as she tugged at Herc's arm. "And you're not really angry, are you?" she added, sensing his thoughts."

"Well—maybe not," replied Herc. "Besides, I am a member of your Lightning League, and I must live up to your motto. What is it again, Jayce?"

Jayce smiled broadly, as he and the others answered together: "'A Courageous Heart, A Righteous Quest.'"